THE SQUINT

Looking through a spy-hole in an old house takes Ben into a thrilling adventure!

Lesley Howarth's books for children include *MapHead*, which won the 1995 Guardian Children's Fiction Award, and *Weather Eye*, which won the Smarties Book Prize (9 – 11 Category). For younger readers she has written *Fort Biscuit*. Her most recent books are *Mister Spaceman* and *Paulina*.

Books by the same author

For younger readers

Fort Biscuit

For older readers

The Flower King
MapHead
MapHead 2
Mister Spaceman
Paulina
The Pits
Weather Eye

LESLEY HOWARTH

Illustrations by

JEFF CUMMINS

WALKER BOOKS
AND SUBSIDIARIES

LONDON • BOSTON • SYDNEY

First published 1998 by Walker Books Ltd
87 Vauxhall Walk, London SE11 5HJ

This edition published 1999

2 4 6 8 10 9 7 5 3

Text © 1998 Lesley Howarth
Illustrations © 1998 Jeff Cummins

This book has been typeset in Plantin.

The right of Lesley Howarth to be identified as author of this
work has been asserted by her in accordance with the
Copyright, Designs and Patents Act 1988.

Printed in Great Britain by The Guernsey Press Co. Ltd

British Library Cataloguing in Publication Data
A catalogue record for this book is
available from the British Library.

ISBN 0-7445-6034-9

Contents

Chapter 1

Cousin Robin

....

"Auntie Heather! Auntie Heather – Ben hit me!"

Cousin Robin stood outside Ben Laker's kitchen window and called to Ben Laker's mother in his best, most earnest, complaining voice. He wanted her to come out *now*. He hadn't got all day.

"Can you come out, Auntie Heather? Only, I think he might do it again!"

Can you come out, Auntie Heather?

Ben watched Robin scornfully. He really was a prat. Ben Laker hadn't, in point of fact, hit his cousin at all. He'd actually pushed Robin once, when Robin had got too annoying. But Cousin Robin wasn't about to let a little thing like the truth get in the way of his whingeing.

"It really hurt, Auntie Heather, and

I wasn't even doing anything!"

He had it off to a fine art, Ben had to admit. The hard-done-by look. The little, wavering voice, so unsure of itself. The way Robin had of not-wanting-to-bother-you, Auntie Heather, *but...*

Ben Laker sighed. How long could half-term *be*? Why in the name of holidays had his mother ever invited Cousin Robin to stay? Ben wished he had a big, bluff dad to throw Cousin Robin in the air – playfully, of course – and wrestle with him really quite roughly, and generally sort him out. But he hadn't, and that was that. Ben's dad was in America, where he'd always been, ever since Ben could first remember asking where he was. Ben didn't even know what he looked like. He might be a weedy dad, for all Ben knew. Like a sort of grown-up Robin. Ben tried to imagine a grown-up Robin. Then he knew his father had to be different. One day he would find out.

Ben's mother came out into the garden.

Ben watched her pegging out washing while Cousin Robin bent her ear about all the things Ben had supposedly done to him – or supposedly planned to do to him – since the last time he'd told her all about it. When Ben's mother had finished she handed Robin the washing basket. Cousin Robin took it dutifully, saving a look for Ben as he went in, a look that said, You've got it coming.

As soon as the door had closed on Robin, Ben's mother shook her head. "Now, Ben," she began, "you know Cousin Robin's our guest – "

Ben eyed the kitchen window. Could Robin earwag through glass?

" – and we have to do our best to entertain him."

"*Why* do we?" Ben burst out. "I *hate* Cousin Robin! He *always* gets his own way!"

"That can't be true, now can it? Be reasonable, Ben," his mother said. "He likes to be the centre of attention, but he isn't staying much longer. Surely you don't have to hit him and take his things."

"I *don't* hit him and take his things!"

"Well, that's how it looks to Robin."

"How about *me*?" Ben felt so indignant, he could hardly get his breath. He hadn't realized – he hadn't known – how far Robin had got round his mother. "How about how it looks to *me*? Maybe I actually want some holidays *without* Cousin Robin. Maybe I don't even *like* him, maybe I—"

"All right, Ben," Ben's mother said firmly. "That'll do." He watched her go in.

She didn't understand. He couldn't do *anything* without Robin. Ben sighed again. Just how long would Cousin Robin need to be entertained? The whole rest of the holiday or something? That's what it looked like to Ben. Hadn't he checked the E.T.D.C.R. (Expected Time of Departure, Cousin Robin) a million times on the calendar in the kitchen? Ben had asked his mother twice if Robin couldn't go earlier. Did he *have* to stay till Saturday? Ben needed peace and quiet, didn't he, to get his holiday project done? He might not get *any homework done at all* if Robin didn't go earlier.

But Cousin Robin's departure date stood firmly at Saturday the twenty-sixth – the end of the week – despite Ben's attempt to cross it out and change it. ROBIN GOES, said the twenty-sixth of May, in his mother's thick red felt-tip. C. ARRIVES? it said also, but Ben didn't know about that.

Nothing could change the day. He was stuck with Robin till Saturday. That left *one day* Robin-free before Ben had to go back to school and his mother back to work, and then the holiday would be over and Robin would have used it all up. If only a plane would crash on darling Robin. If only he, Ben, could fight him with lances and armour, or throw down a glove and meet him with pistols at dawn. Would he *ever* get rid of him? If only his mother could see what Cousin Robin was *really like*.

Ben went into the house and swiftly

upstairs to his room. He shoved the bunk-beds across the door to stop Cousin Robin coming in. Then he switched on the computer. For a long time he played Mortal Kombat. Every character Ben karate-kicked was Cousin Robin. He could hear Cousin Robin whining downstairs.

Enjoying his Robin-free zone, Ben loaded a new game called Gothick. It was a pretty good game, Ben thought. There were castles and knights and their chargers. Soon he reached level six. But before Ben could pin down the Loathly Knight and club out his brains earning three extra lives, his mother called upstairs:

"Ben! Are you up there? How about an outing?"

Ben said guardedly, "Where to?"

"Somewhere you and Robin can get a bit of air!"

That meant a walk, Ben knew.

"We could have a cream tea somewhere – it might take your minds off arguing!"

His mother had made up her mind. Ben shut down the computer and Gothick flickered away. He ejected the disk from the disk-drive and clipped it into its case. GOTHICK – COPYRIGHT MYSTERON GAMES, USA, said the case. Made in America, Ben thought. Where his father was. Where all the best things were.

Pulling on a sweater, he stomped downstairs to the kitchen. Cousin Robin sat smugly waiting, done up in his dorky coat. Robin *would* be ready already. He was probably ready *yesterday*. Never mind – ROBIN GOES said the box for Saturday the twenty-sixth of May on the calendar on the kitchen wall, in glorious red felt-tip letters. ROBIN GOES – C. ARRIVES? Who was C, anyway?

Chapter 2

SEMEL et SEMPER

Once and for Always

....

"Just this once," Ben's mother said. "Come round the House with us – please?"

"I really think you *should*, Ben," Cousin Robin said earnestly – too earnestly, by half. "Don't you *like* historic houses? It's *educational*."

Ben Laker didn't especially like historic houses. He wouldn't have come if he'd known. It wasn't until they were entering the Great Hall at Pentacote House that he'd realized his mother had a *history* lesson in mind.

Pentacote House was just down the road. Ben often walked in the gardens when forced to show visitors around. Usually he showed them the carp pond and the dovecote, then they went round the House, something Ben tried to avoid. He usually managed to slip away and see-off an ice-cream, instead. They did a top blackcurrant ripple down on the Quay. Ben didn't see much point in trailing around on the Historic Pentacote Guided Tour unless you *liked* crumbly old houses filled with paintings and armour and big old echoing halls so cold you could feel your *head* freeze. But today he'd joined the Tour. His mother – and Robin – had insisted.

They entered the Great Hall, so long and tall and empty it felt like a church. A mighty fireplace yawned in the wall – mighty black, it looked, too, Ben thought. Probably they'd just thrown meat on the fire, in the old days. Probably it had got a bit burnt. They probably didn't mind a bit of burnt meat back when they lived in fridges. Probably it was the highlight of their week. He looked around. They hadn't bothered with wallpaper, either. Instead, they'd hung pikes and axes and spiky things all over the walls to cheer everyone up over breakfast. In between hung banners showing shields covered in spots and stripes and castles, with leopards and unicorns and complicated-looking flourishes underneath. Ben looked up. The roof overhead made a criss-cross of ancient timbers. High in the wall was a mysterious hole the shape of a cloverleaf. Instead of telling them what it was *for*, the guide droned on about arms.

"As you'll see," the guide said, "the arms covering the walls of the Great Hall here at Pentacote House date from the fifteenth century – "

"I don't see any arms," Ben said.

" – arms in this case being *family badges*, of course."

Ben looked up at the banners. "You mean those shield things are arms?"

"The arms of the family themselves," the guide went on, "can be found over the grand staircase as you proceed through the—"

"What's that hole in the wall?" Ben asked. "That funny-looking hole, up there?"

The guide looked up at the mysterious

hole. "That's the, ah – the squint."

"What's a squint?" demanded a woman with an American accent. "Would that be something you look through?"

"Exactly." The tour guide pointed. "The cloverleaf hole you'll see high in the wall over there connects the Great Hall with an upper room. A squint was a spyhole for members of the family who didn't wish to dine downstairs."

"Why didn't they?" asked Ben.

"They had their reasons, I suppose." The guide looked at Ben, clearly wishing *he* weren't downstairs either. She went on. "The great fireplace on your right originally held spits for roasting meat."

"Would they have had a pulley system for turning it?" Everyone turned to look at Cousin Robin. Cousin Robin adjusted his glasses. "It's usual," he said. "Apparently."

"That's absolutely right," the tour guide said. "With such large pieces of meat, a pulley system would have been used. They wouldn't simply have thrown meat on the fire."

The tour guide beamed at Robin. He wriggled a bit, in delight. Cousin Robin had got it right. Cousin Robin *would*. It was only because he'd bought the guidebook. Ben felt like hitting him. He really was revolting.

"Here's someone who knows his history." The tour guide hadn't finished with Robin yet. "I wonder if he can tell me the meaning of the family motto *Semel et Semper?*"

"*Semel – et semolina?*" Robin stammered. "It isn't in the book, I mean – is it to do with—"

"Once and for Always," Ben piped up. He didn't know how, but he knew.

"Quite right," the guide said, shortly. "Shall we move on to the kitchens?"

They followed the guide through the pantries, then the dairy, poking things and looking in cupboards and lifting up things they shouldn't, then into the oven-mouthed kitchen, hung with plaster hams, bright with copper pans. The Americans just *loved* it. They said so, all the time.

"And what are those things up there? *Jell-O* moulds? You're kidding!"

"Esme, take a look at this range – isn't it to *die* for?"

Ben liked the way they said things. He especially liked their accents. He liked to think, especially, that his father might talk that way. He had to imagine everything. He didn't know much for certain. Just about the only thing Ben knew for sure about his father was that he lived in America, in a place called *Arkansas*. Ar-kin-saw was a magic place you spelled one way, and said another.

Ben found his mother's arm. "There you are," she said. Then, "How on *earth* did you know what that motto meant? Did you read it in the guidebook, or something?"

"No," Ben said. "I don't know how I knew." After a moment, he said, "You know my dad's in America? You know you said he's been there since I was little?"

"Ye-es," Ben's mother said. "Look at these big copper pans. How did they manage to—"

"Well, can I go and see him?"

"Your dad." Ben's mother looked at him. "What's made you think about him now?"

"I want to see what he looks like. When can I go and visit him, d'you think?"

"I told you. When you're older."

"But I want to visit him *now*."

"You might not have to." Ben's mother flushed. "You never know what might happen."

"But I *want* to. I want to know—"

"When you're ready," the guide announced, "you'll find the library on your *right* as we follow the central passage."

"Come on," Ben's mother said. "Let's see the library now."

The library smelled of old leather. In between listening to stuff about books and bindings and King Charles staying the night (he seemed to have stayed everywhere you went) Ben had plenty of time to think. He

wondered if his father looked like King
Charles, at all. He bet everyone *else* in the
tour party saw their dad. He bet *American*
people never had dads in England *they*
couldn't see. *Why* couldn't he visit his father
now he was ten? Didn't his father *want* him?
How come his father never visited? Never
wrote? Only ever sent him a card or ten bucks
on his birthday? The sound of *ten bucks* was
nice. But it only made the picture of his
father more lonesome, more mysterious,
more intriguing. The only other thing Ben
knew for sure about his dad was that the
night they met, his mother had worn a blue
dress she *still* had hanging in her wardrobe.
Sad, or what? Ben sighed.

Ben stayed behind in the library, when at
last the others wandered on. He felt tired and
fed up. He sat down. Why shouldn't he make
himself at home? Soon the tour guide's voice
died away and the heavy hush of the library
wrapped Ben in its cloak. He probably
shouldn't, but he took down a book anyway,

entitled *Androcles and the Lion*. It wasn't half bad. Ben sat in a leather-backed chair and lost himself in the story. He was glad old Androcles came good in the end, and made a friend of the lion.

When at last he put the book back, Ben found he was quite alone. He ran to the door in a panic. The central passage leading to the hall and the kitchens – and all the rooms branching off it – were cold and bare as winter. There wasn't a sound to be heard.

"Hullo?" Ben called. "Is there anyone there? Mum! Mum! *Where are you?*"

He hadn't meant – he didn't know – where had everyone *gone* to? How long had he been reading? Ten minutes, a quarter – *half* an hour? Hadn't anyone missed him, at all? Hadn't anyone *waited*?

Chapter 3

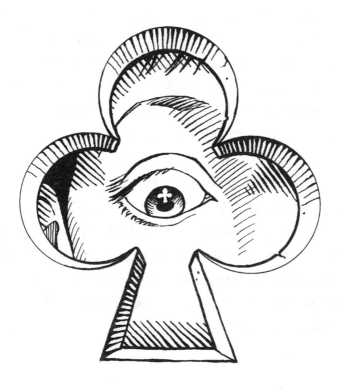

The Squint

Ben raced from room to room. "Mum!" he
called. "Are you in there?"

He walked the length of a long and
mournful gallery, and all the portraits stared
down at him. He made himself walk back
again. The portraits would lift their painted
lips into a painted sneer if he ran. They'd
know they had him rattled. *We know our place
– do you?* they seemed to say. *If you don't even
know your father, what can you be sure of, after
all?* Their eyes followed him accusingly
wherever he went, the same tapestry
greyhounds raced along the same tapestry
hangings, until at last Ben stopped, out of
breath. He was going round in circles. Where
had he started? Where was he going? Would
anyone come to find him?

At last Ben found the staircase. "Mum –

are you up there?" he called.

Fresh portraits sneered at Ben as he climbed the stairs. Black-eyed ladies and feathered lords looked down their noses and whispered to him as he passed: *What can you know? Can you be sure? Who are you really, Ben Laker?* Ben wasn't sure any more. That sword, that dog-whip on the wall, why did he feel he *knew* them? Why did he strongly feel he'd slid down the banisters at some point and hurt himself in the process? And that coat of arms over the staircase, the family coat of arms, with its Latin motto under it which read, *Semel et Semper* – Once and for Always. No one else had known what it meant. *How* had he known what it meant?

Then there was the painting over the stairs. Ben Laker looked up at the lady in blue with her pale son standing beside her, just about his age. It seemed to Ben she had the face of someone he might have seen in a dream that he wasn't enjoying, a dream in which she looked like someone else, but really he *knew* who she was. Suddenly frightened, Ben ran up the stairs. Taking them two at a time, topping them too suddenly and falling over himself, he ran *slap-bang* into a suit of armour that waited in the shadows.

It felt horrible. Instead of falling over, the suit of armour bowed. Its helmet nodded, its jaw dropped, its arms fell down around Ben. It was *hugging* him! He couldn't get out – he *had* to! Furiously Ben ducked away, throwing off its cold arms, its metal breath of battles. He mustn't panic. There was no one inside it. It was just a suit of armour.

There had to be someone else in the House. Pretty soon he'd bump into them. He ran down a long, dark corridor, then lightly through several rooms. But no matter how many times he called, no one answered back; and no matter how hard he listened, his were the only feet to make the floorboards creak. Finally he reached a room with a strangely shaped hole in the wall. The hole caught his eye straight away. It looked, Ben thought, like the clubs in a pack of cards. It drew him into the room as soon as he saw it.

It was quite a small room, really. It had white-washed walls and creaking oak beams for a floor, a bed, a chair – and the hole. The hole in the wall reminded Ben of the cloverleaf squint in the Great Hall downstairs for about a second before he realized that that was exactly what it was. He was looking at the squint *from the other side this time*, the side where the family had hidden when they hadn't wanted to dine with everyone else.

The squint was quite small, about the size of Ben's hand, and each of its cloverleaf holes would give you a slightly different view over the Great Hall far below – and would hide your eye while you were squinting through it, to see what you might see. You could spy on people, Ben realized, and *no one could see who was spying*.

His panic forgotten, Ben put his eye to the squint. Perhaps he'd spy his mother, the tour guide, *anyone*. Even that suck-up Robin would look pretty good, at that moment.

Ben shivered as the cold, cold stone of the squint touched his face. It had touched his face here before, and not only his, but Maudlin's. *Maudlin?* Ben thought, *Who's Maudlin?* The draught through the squint seemed to blow him her name. The air in this room was deathly cold, colder than anywhere else. Why, Ben wondered, would anyone *want* to stay up here in the freezing cold when they might've been roasting their faces in front of the fire? The tour guide had said the family had had their reasons. What *were* their reasons? he wondered.

In the moment he looked down, he knew. Through the clover-shaped squint high in the wall of the Great Hall at Pentacote, Ben watched the feast far below. He felt as though he'd watched there many times before. A murmuring rose up and filled the timbered roof-space. Smoke spiralled up from the hearth. The fire itself was out of Ben's sight, but from his viewpoint at the squint he could make out every expression on every face, every snub or shrug, every wink or hint, every single thing every single person ate. It really was a secret place to watch. Somehow he knew Aunt Maudlin had watched from this secret spyhole in her bedroom wall, as well – and he knew she hadn't watched because she'd wanted to. It wasn't because Maudlin didn't wish to dine downstairs. It was because she wasn't *allowed* to.

Maudlin had felt very angry when she watched the Hall below. Immediately Ben looked through the squint he felt pretty angry himself. Long trestles lined with people in medieval clothes filled the Hall, but it was the top table – the *family* table – Ben couldn't take his eyes off, the table that made him so angry, the table he should have been *at*. Incredibly, there was *someone else* in his place at the head of the table. Who was that petting his favourite hound? Taking *his* seat at the head of the table, next to – next to *his mother* dressed all in black?

Mum – is that you? Who's that sitting next to you? Who does he think he is?

Ben felt angry and frustrated. Whose feelings were these, anyway? Maudlin must have felt this way, Ben thought. Aunt Maudlin had thought she would marry, and leave this room for good. But someone had stood in her way. Someone she hated very much.

Someone *Ben* hated very much was the person who'd taken his place at the head of the table. The person, whoever it was, was obviously annoying his mother. His mother didn't like it at all, Ben could see. She tried turning to someone else, but the person taking Ben's place only tugged her arm and made her turn back to him again. Ben longed to tell him off. Couldn't he *see* he was boring her? Couldn't he leave her alone?

Suddenly Ben got up. Leaving Aunt Maudlin's door ajar, he ran back the way he'd come, not wondering *how* he knew what he knew, just *knowing* it in his bones, the way he knew his way to the head of the staircase, the way he knew the Lakesbeare family motto – Once and for Always – the way he knew the banisters would support him.

He ran past the lady in blue with her pale son standing beside her, the portrait – he remembered it now – of himself and his mother in her favourite blue dress that the artist had put the finishing touches to the *very day* his poor father had been tragically killed in the hunt; the day before Uncle Renald and Robyn, his slimy son, had arrived with all their servants. He ran past the arms of Lakesbeare over the staircase – a white greyhound supporting gold bars on a silver field. Past his father's suit of armour in the shadows at the top of the stairs – the armour that had tried, and failed, to hug him on the way up.

Ben reached the old oak banisters. He swung himself onto them, the way he'd done a hundred times before, including the time he fell off once and almost split his head on the stones below. That was then. This was now. But nothing much had changed. Once and for Always, Ben thought, *that's right*. And slid all the way into his past.

Chapter 4

Below the Salt

Ben Lakesbeare entered the Great Hall with as much dignity as he could muster, after sliding down the banisters in a rage.

"A Lakesbeare!" he cried on entering, the way the family always did.

A hush fell. At the other end of the Hall, where the Lakesbeare family sat around the top table together, someone dropped a dish. *As well they might*, Ben thought. With the top table well in his sights – and everyone sitting at it – it was clear to everyone, especially to Ben, who'd taken his rightful place. Ben hadn't recognized him from the squint. *Now* he could see who it was.

Now it was clear that it was *Cousin Robyn* who'd taken his place at the head of the table, *Cousin Robyn* who was boring his, Ben's, mother to death, *Cousin Robyn* who was pestering her with questions, probably questions about the Estate he had no business asking. *Sweet* Cousin Robyn, as everyone called him. It was enough to make Ben's blood boil. As if Cousin Robyn and his father, Uncle Renald, cared about anyone but themselves. Hadn't they turned up the *night after* Ben's father died in a hunting accident, when they hadn't been near the place in years? Now *sweet* Cousin Robyn was putting on airs. Dressing richly. Buying a horse. Fondling Cygnus, Ben's favourite dog. Taking his, Ben's, seat at the head of the table.

Ben marched coldly across the Hall, straight towards Cousin Robyn. Several of his father's old servants stopped eating to watch him pass, so closely did his ringing step remind them of his father's. Cousin Robyn had seen him coming, Ben felt sure. But still he pretended not to notice. How *dare* he take Ben's place? As heir to his newly dead father, pride of place was *his*.

Ben stood before the salt. Never taking his eyes from Cousin Robyn, he skirted the glittering bowl of salt – so rare and expensive it sat on a table on its own – and bounded up to take his place at the raised table above it. The family always sat above the salt. The salt was a sign of the lord's wealth and power. No one belonging to the family ever dined below it.

"Cygnus – here!" Ben reached his chair. Not only did Cousin Robyn fill it, he also had Ben's favourite dog at his feet. "Cygnus!" Ben scolded. "Come to me then, swan" – her name meant *swan*.

Ben's favourite white greyhound got up, smiling all over her chops. And not before time, Ben thought, forgiving her straight away. Cygnus was young and easily led. She'd fawn over anyone giving her titbits, even over loathsome Cousin Robyn, more loathsome today than usual, despite his sumptuous new clothes. Ben took in Cousin Robyn's expensive red velvet suit, not the first he'd had lately. No wonder he'd failed to recognize his cousin from the squint. So gorgeous were Cousin Robyn's velvet coat and hat, his gormless face would have been lost in them unless he'd folded them back. All that red velvet made him look ridiculous, Ben thought. It didn't suit him at all. He looked like an apple with a worm in it. Who did he think he was, the Lord of the Manor?

"Admiring my velvet?" Robyn asked. "Too *rich* for you, I should think. Not *quite* the Lakesbeare style, I don't suppose."

Too rich, Ben thought. *You got that right.*

"You don't have much style at Pentacote, do you?" Robyn needled. "You are so *rural.*"

"*Down,* swan," Ben told his dog. He turned, at last, to Cousin Robyn. "How now, Coz?" he said.

"How now?" Perfect Cousin Robyn furrowed his perfect brow. "What's 'how now' supposed to mean?"

"It means," Ben said, "how come you're still in my seat?"

"*Your* seat?" Robyn snorted. "This is the family table, I think?" He waved his knife at the trestles below. "Plenty of empty seats below the salt."

"Only fools and peasants sit below it."

Robyn raised an eyebrow. "And which," he asked Ben, "are you?"

"You think you're so clever," Ben said. "One day I'll fight you properly. One day I'll beat you at something – " Ben set a hand on Cousin Robyn's chair " – and *then* you'll know whose place this is, once and for all."

Cousin Robyn flinched. Only the very lowest tables were eating. Everyone else was listening. His father, Renald, signalled *Say something* impatiently. Ben Lakesbeare had practically challenged him. He, Robyn, *had* to respond. The trouble was, he couldn't think of anything to say.

"My goshawk, Amica, will peck out your eyes if you hit me," he said sniffily, at last.

"I'll push in your chest in the tilt-yard," Ben said.

"If I ever *went* in the tilt-yard."

"I'll fight you with muffled lances."

Cousin Robyn examined his nails. "And if I win?"

"I'll step down and *you* take my place. And if *I* win—"

"Can you pass me the wine?" Robyn asked rudely. "If you don't mind. I thank you."

Ben fought an urge to pour the flagon of wine over Cousin Robyn's head. Instead, he said, "And if *I* win, I take your new horse."

"My lovely black Lascar? I don't think so."

"I'll fight you and I'll win and I'll take your black horse *off* you."

"My," Cousin Robyn said archly, "if only the Lord of the Manor would let you *try*. Which of us looks more *like* a lord, d'you think?"

Cousin Robyn, Lord of the Manor? As if. Ben Lakesbeare almost knocked his cousin down, there and then. Wasn't *he*, Ben Lakesbeare, heir of Pentacote? On the eve of his twelfth birthday he'd spend the night in the family chapel, in vigil over his father's arms and armour, then next day he would be entitled to wear them – and *then* he'd be the Lord of the Manor. The sticky bit was between then and now. Uncle Renald knew it, too. Until the eve of his twelfth birthday – if he survived that long, with a grasping uncle for a guardian – until the eve of his twelfth birthday, Ben's Uncle Renald would run the Estate and *there was nothing Ben Lakesbeare could do about it*. If anything happened to Ben, then – and only then – would Cousin Robyn take his place as Fourth – as *Fifth* Earl of Pentacote. Unthinkable, but Ben thought it. It seemed Cousin Robyn had, too.

Ben glanced up at the squint. Was that the glitter of an eye?

Aunt Maudlin, he thought, *are you watching? I know you can see what they're up to. We've got to stick together, you and me. They want to send you away so you can't get married. Now they want me out of the way, as well.*

Only minutes before, from Maudlin's side

of the squint and a distance of five hundred years, Ben had longed to wipe the smile from Cousin Robyn's face. Now Ben found he could do nothing but watch, with barely controlled anger, as Cousin Robyn coolly peeled a quince with his knife. What would his father have said? If only he were here to sort Robyn out. Couldn't his mother at least *do* something? This was her House, too. Ben searched the table for his mother – where had she gone? – and found her laughing with Uncle Renald.

"Hebe! You'll be the death of me!" Renald laughed, with food coming out of his mouth.

If only she would, Ben thought. How could she joke with Uncle Renald? Couldn't she see what Renald and Robyn were up to? Had she gone blind since she'd folded away her blue dress – the blue dress his father had liked especially – the morning after his father's hunting accident?

Ben's mother returned to her seat beside Cousin Robyn. She hid her pale face in her hands. Then she turned to Robyn and put on a smile. "Your father tells me the hunt is on tomorrow?"

"That's right." Cousin Robyn reached rudely across his aunt for more fruit. "My goshawk, Amica, will show her colours, I think." He paused. "She may even tear down a Lakesbeare bird or two – should you like that, Aunt Hebe, I wonder?" He watched her closely as he said it.

"She may, I suppose." Ben's mother laughed. "Sweet Cousin Robyn," she said.

Ben watched his mother's face. Her laugh had sounded strained, as though it had taken all her strength to find anything amusing in what sweet Cousin Robyn had to tell her. Still she would be amused. Still she would be dear Aunt Hebe, friend to Cousin Robyn, until she saw what was going to happen. Suddenly Ben saw that his mother was afraid. Deathly afraid. So afraid, she was laughing.

Chapter 5

Unc Tewus

"I don't know *how* you got lost," Ben's mother complained. "We were only out in the gardens."

"Well, I did, and I wish I hadn't." Ben felt really stirred up. "Anyway – we're home now."

"*Terribly* interesting place," Robin said as the car pulled in. "Wasn't it, Auntie Heather?"

As soon as they got in, Robin started his homework. Ben curled his lip and put on the telly. Cousin Robin *would*. Doing your half-term project mid-week, when you didn't even have to. Sad, or what? No way would Ben do his till the day before they went back.

It had been, Cousin Robin informed Ben's mother as she peeled potatoes for tea, it had been an *extremely fortunate outing*. It just so happened that his history project involved the Middle Ages. It just so happened that the guidebook he'd got at Pentacote would be brilliant to cut up and label. It would beat the stuffing – Robin looked at his aunt to see the effect he was making – it would beat the *stuffing* out of Claire Rollins at school. Claire Rollins usually got top marks, but this time she wouldn't get a look-in.

"Well," Ben's mother smiled, "you've certainly got a head start. I'm really glad we went."

"So am *I*, Auntie Heather," Robin slimed. "Thanks a million for taking us. I love old houses and history. Don't you love old houses and history, Ben?"

"Mad for 'em," Ben said.

Ben hated the way his mother couldn't see what Cousin Robin was *like*. Far from being meek and mild, the way he liked to play it with any adults around, Cousin Robin was pretty competitive. Pretty ruthless, in fact. All those wheedling lies he told. Ben was seriously thinking of setting up a camcorder in the bedroom he – reluctantly – shared with Robin. How else could he protect himself from all the stories about kicks and thumps and pinches he'd supposedly dealt him, that *dear*, darling Robin told his mother about behind his back?

"What's *unctuous* mean?" Ben asked suddenly, over *The Six O'Clock News*. The politicians on screen had just had a go at one another. Why couldn't they use words people could *understand*? Unc-tu-ous. Unc-tewus. It sounded like a Deep South kind of uncle, the sort that hung around chewing baccy and told you, Never go look in the woodpile.

"Unctuous…" Robin flicked through the dictionary, practically drooling over it now someone had actually asked him to look up a word. He loved showing off, he really did.

"Unctuous, unctuous, unctuous – here we are. It means someone who's oily, greasy, smug, gushing. Someone affecting – or pretending – sincerity, earnestness or enthusiasm."

Oily. Greasy. Smug. Gushing. Ben watched Cousin Robin enthusiastically describing himself.

"Exactly," Ben said darkly.

By teatime things were worse. Tension built over sausage and chips to the point where anything, no matter how small, was going to trigger an explosion. Robin had started complaining again, in his still, small I-didn't-really-want-to-mention-it-*but* voice. Ben felt annoyed. Didn't his mother realize? There was nothing wrong with Robin. Robin was just being a pain. Already Ben had had to listen while Cousin Robin wound his mother up over things that might possibly go wrong with him in the night. He was delicate, you see. Ordinary fabrics could upset him. Ben's duvet would probably suit him better than the one he had on his bed. Ben's pillows, too. Foam was so much better. Feathers could give him a sniffle, if anything got up his nose.

Ben Laker knew what got up *his* nose, and it wasn't a million miles from the sad sack at the head of the table. Where *he* usually sat, Ben noticed.

Suddenly Ben leaned over. "Can you pass the salt, if it's not too much trouble?"

Robin regarded him coldly. Already he'd sniggered when Ben had accidentally tipped a flood of ketchup over his sausages.

"Sure you can handle it?" he asked.

"Now, boys." Ben's mother got up and went out to the kitchen to look at a pudding. Conditions were perfect for an explosion. All that was needed was a spark.

Robin got up. "How about if I do it for you?" He waved the salt out of Ben's reach. "We wouldn't want you spoiling your dinner."

Ben lunged for the saltcellar, but Robin wasn't about to give it up. Suddenly they were grappling with each other. Ben was bigger, but Robin was surprisingly slippery. Finally Ben wrenched the saltcellar out of his cousin's hand and joyfully unscrewed it over his cousin's meal, tipping the rest of the salt down his cousin's neck, just as his mother re-entered the room. Ben's mother took in the scene. Cousin Robin composed his face. He was going to enjoy this a lot.

"Auntie Heather, Ben just put salt down my neck!"

Ben's mother set down pudding plates and took up Robin's meal. The meal that was drowned in salt.

"*And* he just poured salt all over my sausages and now I can't even eat them, and I really *love* sausages, Auntie Heather, and I don't even know why he did it."

Ben had to admit, it looked bad. About as bad as it could look. "Mum," he said, "I didn't mean to do it – it's just that he's so *annoying*."

"I don't expect this from you, Ben." Ben's mother looked at him sternly. "Go to your room now," she said.

That night in bed Ben got out the last ten

bucks his mysterious father had sent him. His mother had wanted the interesting-looking note changed at the bank so that Ben could spend it. But Ben never wanted to spend it. He looked at the picture of some old man in a fussy wing collar on the front of the ten dollar bills. Did his father look like that? Or was he square-jawed and square-built, a bit like a gladiator? If he was, what would he be called? Robin-masher. That would be good. Rob-o-cuter, even better. Or maybe Eliminator. Ben sighed. Probably even his father couldn't get rid of Cousin Robin.

I don't expect this from you, Ben. His mother had looked really hurt. That was what was so maddening. Robin was undermining him. The maddening thing was, it was working.

Later Robin would come up to bed and go on and *on* about the fight over tea, and how much it had upset Auntie Heather. As if he cared. Ben was certain he didn't. He considered Robin's bunk-bed and thought about putting something sticky or smelly or both in it, but he couldn't be bothered, in the end. What was the point? Robin would only go whining downstairs and things would be even worse.

Ben lay back and felt sleepy. At least he'd got Robin at teatime. Putting salt down Cousin Robin's neck had felt *really good* at the time. It was wrong, Ben knew, to throw salt around on the floor. Salt was fetching a tremendous price, lately – all of thirty hides to secure a *single firkin*. At a price like that, the bowl in the Great Hall held practically a king's ransom. Practically all Aunt Maudlin's dowry, at least.

Renald had put away the dowry. He said Maudlin should go to a convent instead, because the person she wanted to marry wasn't good enough for her. He wanted to keep the dowry money for himself and not have to pay it to Maudlin's new husband's family after the wedding, anybody could see. Aunt Maudlin had taken it badly. Keep to your room, Renald said. She didn't need any telling. She spent all her time locked away. Everything would be different once he, Ben Lakesbeare, came of age. Poor Maudlin would do as she liked. He would find a cheaper source of salt. Stop Cousin Robyn buying clothes. The Estate would have to pull in its belt, at least until this time next year. There were many things he would have to consider, as Lord of the Lakesbeare Estates, many responsibilities he would have to shoulder, not least the supply of salt.

Ben sat up. What in the – medieval – world was he thinking about? Estates, what estates? He had Aunt Maudlin, whoever she was, on the brain. Why was he worrying about the *supply of salt*, of all things? He guessed there'd be enough Saxo in Safeway to tide them over for about the next decade or two. He should worry. The only problem he had on his mind was escaping dear Robbo next morning.

Chapter 6

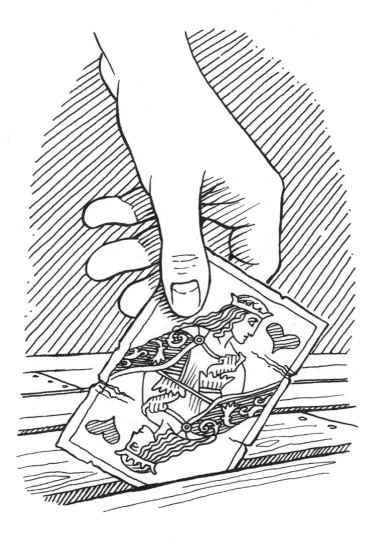

Poor Maudlin

Next morning Ben knew straight away that he was going back to Pentacote, no question. He ducked Robin's questions, then his mum's. He rang Marky Swanson early, and his friend rang him back at a pre-arranged time. He was good that way, was Marky. Ben would do the same for him. He only had to ask.

Ben made sure he picked up the phone when it rang. "Marky Swanson says, can I go over for the day?" he asked his mother. "Well, can I? I won't be late."

At half-past nine that morning, Ben Laker set off on his bike. It didn't take him long. Instead of going to Marky's house, he rode straight down the road to Pentacote. At exactly twenty to ten, Ben turned in on the gravel drive and crunched his way up to the

House. Past Pentacote Barn, where they did a top cream tea, past the carved stone arms of the Lakesbeares over the gate, weathered into vague-looking lumps since they were carved and put up, Ben remembered, in 1485. It was happening again. He was remembering things he never could've seen in the *first* place. But it seemed so real. Was he flipping out? Had he read it somewhere, and forgotten? Or was he slipping on *someone else's feelings* again, like the last time he came to the House? Ben parked his bike and felt funny. He felt funny every time he came here. So many questions, every time. Every time he came here.

Ben walked into the courtyard. With his ringing step so like his father's, all Pentacote's windows looked down and seemed to see in Ben someone they saw once before. Ben looked up at the old stone walls. He loved the place, what else was there to know?

GREAT HALL OPEN – PLEASE COME IN, said the sign by the open front door.

Ben walked in at the old oak door. The old oak door he'd torn off his boots behind a hundred times before, the door where Cygnus greeted him, the door – the door his father had come through for the very last time the day he died, to lie in state in the Great Hall under the squint. *The squint,* Ben thought. All that stuff about Lord of the Manor and feasting and tilt-yards and fighting your cousin if you wanted. He'd *had* to come back to see more – who wouldn't? – even though some things upset him.

Ben reached the Admissions desk with a start. With an effort, he brought out his mother's Country Heritage Membership Card and presented it with a smile.

"My mum," he said, "she's just coming…"

The kindly looking woman on the desk wore tweedy clothes and greying, swept-up hair. She looked at Ben in a tweedy, kindly way. "Would you like a guidebook?" she asked.

"Got one," Ben said, going in.

Once more, Ben climbed the stairs to the squint. But first he examined the suit of armour he'd run into the day before. WORN BY EDWARD LAKESBEARE, EARL OF PENTACOTE, BORN 1450, DIED 1485, said the sign between its scaly armoured feet. *Must have been a tall man,* Ben thought, *my father – Edward Lakesbeare, I mean – the man who wore the armour. Funny how his suit of armour hugged me. That's what it felt like, at least.*

He reached the portrait at the stairhead. *She's pretty,* Ben thought, *my mother – the woman in blue in the picture, who looks a bit like my mum, I mean.* Thoroughly confused about who, what and where he was and what he was supposed to be doing, Ben finally reached Aunt Maudlin's room. The room with the squint in the wall.

This time there was a man there – a man wearing a jacket with leather elbow-patches and horn-rimmed glasses and a tie with little oak trees on it. "I'm the steward," he said, "can I help you?"

Ben looked around. Straight away he felt cross. He hadn't planned on a steward. A steward might muck things up, and spoil the atmosphere completely. He wanted to look through the squint, to see what he could see. But he didn't dare, with the steward there. The steward might think he was weird.

"I'd like to look around," Ben said, astonishing himself. "I'd like to be on my own." Suddenly he felt he had a *right* to be on his own. Didn't they trust him, or something? "I'm not going to take anything," he said. "You don't have to watch me, you know."

The steward held up his hands, smiling despite Ben's rudeness. "That's quite all right," he said. "I understand. I'll be in the next room if you want to ask me any questions about the House."

"Sorry," Ben said, "I didn't mean to sound cross."

"You're not the only one," the steward said. "Maudlin's room makes people angry. You wouldn't believe the things people say.

Especially when they look through the squint – the spyhole, over there, in the wall?"

"I know about the squint," Ben said. "But who did Maudlin want to marry?"

"You know about Maudlin, do you?" The steward sighed. "I'm afraid she was unhappy in this room. That's why it makes people angry."

"*Aunt* Maudlin," Ben corrected.

"Sister to Edward Lakesbeare," the steward agreed. "She was to have married William Brookland of Brooklands House – but after her brother's death I'm afraid it fell through."

"But didn't she marry him in the end?" Ben asked. "After – Ben Lakesbeare took over?"

"Records show nothing after 1485. We simply don't know what happened," the steward told Ben. "Shall I leave you to it? I'm next door if you want me."

Ben looked round the comfortless white-washed room. The draught coming in through the squint blew new thoughts into his mind. Probably the room hadn't been white at all, in Maudlin's time. Probably the walls had been stonework, with a tapestry or two, if she was lucky. Which she wasn't, of course. Poor Maudlin was only sixteen when Renald ordered her to stay in her room until he could send her away, when he stopped her marrying William, because he wanted her dowry for himself. How she must have hated him. The way this room – this *House* – felt, had everything to do with poor Maudlin.

On an impulse, Ben stooped down. There – between the floorboards – the edge of a playing card. Ben tweaked it out. Incredible. The queen of hearts smiled up at him. She must have slipped between the floorboards after a game and stayed there for five hundred years, and no one had pulled her out before because no one had dreamed she was there – *another* thing he knew about this House, this room, without knowing how he knew it. But there she was. The queen of hearts had slept between the floorboards since Ben Lakesbeare's last game of cards with poor Aunt Maudlin. He remembered now. He often slipped up to comfort her in her lonely room over the Hall.

A noise below drew Ben's eyes. He pressed his eye to the squint. Far below, in the Great Hall, the hawking party was gathering – was very nearly *ready*. A servant knocked the fire into life, so that it jumped and blazed in the hearth. Hebe offered the huntsmen warm ale and bread, cheese and rings of dried apple. Soon they would ride to hunt rabbits and hares, songbirds, quail and partridge, and anything else the hawks might seize in the air or fall on like an arrow. It wasn't nice, but it did put food on the table. And it exercised the hawks. Ben Lakesbeare kept a hawk. His servant, Owen, came in with it.

"Stryke!" Ben heard himself saying. *"She doesn't like the fire – Owen, take her outside!"*

Owen hooded Stryke and calmed her wings. Renald entered the Hall, closely followed by the Master of Ferrets with his sacks and gloves and leads. The Master of Ferrets was important. His ferrets flushed out rabbits, stoats, weasels, badgers, hares – anything that lived underground – from their holes. No one could go hawking without him.

"Ready?" Renald roared.

"Ready!" the Hall roared back.

"Go to it, then!" he told them, throwing open the great oak doors on the early morning outside. "And the devil take the hindmost!"

Hurry, hurry, hurry. Devil take the hindmost. Everywhere men pulled on boots and spurs. Ben felt excitement leap in his throat. He had only to walk downstairs to join the hunt of his life.

Chapter 7

The Hunt

*It was a hot day, and there weren't many rabbits
above ground. As we rode on towards a warren
we knew, we disturbed a lot of young hogs which
jumped up in front of us and disappeared into the
woodland.* Ben Lakesbeare rehearsed his
account of the hunt as he rode. He had a
feeling he may have to account for anything
and everything he said and did that day.

The day had started badly. He'd joined the
hunt in a hurry, and everything had got
mixed up. For some reason he'd been given
the dim-witted Dugdale to ride. Not only a
stupid horse, Dugdale was nervous, as well.
Ben's female goshawk, Stryke, bobbed
uneasily on his arm. She didn't like Dugdale,
either. It wasn't long since Owen, Ben's boy,
had fetched Stryke from her quarters and
swung her out over the meadows in the

early-morning mist to stretch her wings and sinews. Straining ahead with her keen eyes, now she was ready for some sport. Which was more than Ben was. Weren't these the very hunting grounds – the very woods and marches – that had seen the death of his father? Ben felt the heart go out of him already, and the day had yet to begin.

Already he and Dugdale were getting left behind. Ben spurred his horse – Duggie, come *on* – but Dugdale laid back his ears. With a drum and a rush, a sleek black stallion sped past – beautiful Lascar, dark as a berry, swift as the fall of the arrow. Cousin Robyn turned in the saddle.

"Shall we" – he screamed – "shall we *hunt*?" Lascar tore on. "Shall we hunt? Or shall we just *dawdle*?"

Ben did his best. Finally Dugdale broke into a reluctant gallop, looking fearfully around as he went. At last they caught up. The men had dismounted and organized themselves into a beating and a hawking party by the time Ben arrived on the scene. Cousin Robyn had disappeared. Where had Lascar taken him? Far away, Ben hoped. Meanwhile, there was game afoot. And everywhere, signs of rabbits.

The Master of Ferrets stepped up. This was his moment. He might not be popular – he and his ferrets smelled disgusting – but the hunt wouldn't happen without him. Importantly, he opened one of his sacks and the smell grew even stronger. Reaching inside it with a heavily gloved hand, he drew out a ferret, its eyes red with panic and hate.

Soon, Ben rehearsed, *soon we came to a spot where there were signs of rabbits everywhere. Choosing a likely hole, the Master of Ferrets put a ferret down it. I stood well back, holding Stryke in readiness for a flight.*

In readiness for a flight, I stood well back. Ben ran over and over it. What happened next wasn't easy to cxplain. Ben wondered why the Master of Ferrets had positioned himself opposite the rabbit-hole. He usually kept well away, or the rabbits wouldn't come out.

We hadn't long to wait, Ben recorded. *A rabbit bolted out, and at once I slipped Stryke from my arm. But the rabbit, smelling the Master of Ferrets, instead of bolting straight away, suddenly turned sharp to one side and doubled back, through the midst of our party.*

Straight through the midst of our party. With Stryke, like a falling knife, behind it.

After that, all Ben remembered was horses plunging left and right in panic – someone shouting, someone falling, someone else slapping his horse, Dugdale bolting away through the woods in terror, then rushing branches overhead and a crazy ride over stumps and bumps and hollows that, somehow, Dugdale avoided. Until something much worse stopped him dead.

Stupid old Dugdale – did you have to panic so completely? Didn't you see that massive great branch over the path? The branch that seemed to tremble, then jump out at Ben at a million miles an hour? Didn't you glimpse the red velvet glove that cut the rope holding it back, moments before the branch hit you? Didn't you know, couldn't you see, *that branch had been weighted and sprung like a trap* – a trap waiting just for you?

The branch whipped Ben from his saddle as though he were made of paper. As Ben hit the ground and bit birch leaves, he thought he saw something red – a flash in the leaves, a red leather boot against moss. Red and livid green – Cousin Robyn's colours. Cousin Robyn's riding boots. Cousin Robyn's red velvet gloves as he stooped to pick something up. Ben closed his eyes. Above him he heard the mew of a hawk. Somewhere, way above him, Stryke was mewing as she circled, wondering where his arm was, where the chickens' heads were that he always rewarded her with. She wanted home and a feed. No one, especially not Ben, would hood Stryke and feed her tonight.

Footsteps in the leaves. Ben could only listen.

"Well, well," someone said lightly. "Another one bites the dust."

Someone laughed. Ben held his breath. *This isn't funny,* he thought. No one would deliberately knock you off your horse, knowing you might be killed, then laugh about it afterwards. It wasn't the sort of laugh that knew you were all right, really. It wasn't the sort of laugh to pick you up and carry you home over its saddle. It was a laugh that cared for nothing and no one but itself. Cousin Robyn's laugh.

"These Lakesbeares," the laugher said, lightly. *"How easily they fall."*

These Lakesbeares? *Father,* Ben thought, *are you listening? Is this what happened to you?*

At last the footsteps retreated. Still Ben waited, until he was certain they'd gone. Then he let out a long breath. He wasn't badly injured, only stunned. He'd done the right thing in playing dead. No telling what those red leather boots might do if they thought you might get up and run.

Following the scattering of our party, my horse bolted into the surrounding woodland, where I had the misfortune to strike my head on a branch, Ben recorded dimly, for the record. *At least, I think I did.* Then he let his head fall back into the leaves.

He wasn't as well as he'd thought. The last thing Ben remembered were feathers drifting downwards. Overhead, the goshawks were fighting. Locked together, tumbling through the sky – Ben could see them now – sometimes breaking and lunging, claws and beaks flashing, first one on top and then the other, it had to be Stryke and Amica. Both female, both good hunters, they would probably fight to the death. What had Cousin Robyn said? *My goshawk, Amica, may tear down a Lakesbeare bird or two? Should you like that, Aunt Hebe, I wonder?*

Stryke, Ben thought, *it's up to you. You can't let them win – not now. Fight with every breath in your body. Live up to your name. Strike back for all of us, if you can.*

Chapter 8

Burning Ears

On Cousin Robin's last night, not his last
night ever – Ben wished – but his last night
with Ben and his mum, they all went out for
a meal. Pentacote Barn did Candlelit
Dinners. But nothing seemed to please
Robin.

First, his drink wasn't right. He wanted
apple *perry*, not apple *juice*. Apple juice might
upset him. Once he was up all night. After
they got his drink right, next he kicked up
about cheese.

"The lasagne's nice," Ben's mother said.
"They make it with lots of cheese."

"I can't have too much cheese," Robin
sniffed. "Too much cheese might upset me."

If only it would, Ben thought. If only he
could stick Robin's head in the cheesepress
and press out all the rubbish – except there'd

be nothing left.

He actually knew what a cheesepress was these days – they'd made their own cheese in 1485 – mainly because he couldn't stop thinking as, and about, Ben Lakesbeare, following his fall at the hunt.

Nothing Ben's mother talked about over dinner seemed to matter half as much. Of all things, she talked about Ben's father. Normally, Ben would've pricked up his ears. His mother *never* talked about his father, but tonight, for some reason, she couldn't stop. She told Ben how they'd met; what an interesting man he was; how it wasn't his fault they'd parted; how *good* it would be to get to know him – wouldn't it? – after all this time.

"*My* dad's a chemical engineer," Robin said. "*My* dad's really clever."

"I know he is," Ben's mum said. "You're lucky to have him," she said.

Ben let it all float over him. Life through the squint seemed more real, somehow, than life this side of the cloverleaf hole in the wall.

Already Ben's thoughts were wandering down the darkened drive to the House. It would be closed up, of course, after hours. Edward Lakesbeare's suit of armour would guard an empty staircase. The squint would look down on the empty Great Hall – or would it?

Ben Laker admired his mother through the candlelight. Tonight she looked really nice. Her eyes sparkled. She'd done up her hair. She looked a bit medieval, with her hair twisted up that way.

He wondered what she was thinking. She'd been a long time on the phone last night. She'd sounded quite excited. *Don't say too much now, she'd said. It costs too much over the phone. Say it when I see you. See you tomorrow night.* Tomorrow night – that was tonight.

"Are you going somewhere, after?" Ben asked his mum.

"After what?"

"After we get home. Only, I don't want a

babysitter or anything. I – we – can look after ourselves."

"Oh, I know that." Ben's mother smiled. She was humouring him, Ben knew. She really was mysterious this evening. She looked, well, younger somehow. Maybe it was the blue dress. Blue really suited Ben's mum.

"Why have you got that dress on?" he asked.

"This old thing?" his mother looked down as though she'd only just noticed her old blue dress. "I don't know. Just a thought."

It looked OK, Ben thought. She'd kept it so long in the wardrobe, it had just about got back in fashion.

Ben ate his meal. The meal was good. So were the drinks and the ice-cream. But something was giving him stomachache. Something was burning him deep inside, like hurtful words he couldn't forget. *Someone was saying things about him – things that he knew weren't true.*

"Your ears are pink," Ben's mother said.

"Someone talking about you?"

"I'm sorry?" Ben looked up.

"They're just about on fire," Cousin Robin added. "Making him deaf, I should think."

"You look a bit hot."

"I'm fine."

"Would you like me to top up your drink?"

All at once, Ben stood up. "No thanks," he said. "I think I'll go to the toilet."

Once in the outside passage, Ben turned right instead of left. Instead of coming out by the toilets, he popped out onto the darkened drive and crunched his way down to the House.

Under the stone coat of arms, with its motto – Once and for Always – still visible if you knew where to look for it; across the cobbled courtyard, where the ivy-fringed windows looked down and expected his every step; up to the old oak door, which opened for him as he reached it. Ben Lakesbeare stepped boldly inside. And into the fire-lit Great Hall.

They were all there, above the salt. Renald, Hebe, Maudlin, Ben's body-servant Owen, the chief stewards of the Estate, Master of Ferrets included. Oh, and *sweet* Cousin Robyn. Cygnus came smiling to meet him. The only one who did.

Uncle Renald turned as Ben entered. His mother covered her mouth.

"So," Renald said, "at last. You come to answer the charges."

"I *knew* he would." Aunt Maudlin lit up. "My only friend. I *told* you he'd come," she said.

Chapter 9

The Charges

"He tried to kill me," Robyn said, "and I don't know *why*, Aunt Hebe. As soon as the rabbit came out of the hole, he rode me down and crushed me."

"What do you mean, I tried to kill you?" Ben Lakesbeare demanded. He'd just walked into the Great Hall, and they'd all stared down at him as if he'd just come back from the dead. Now Cousin Robyn was saying that he, Ben, had tried to kill him – and everyone was actually *listening* to him. "I don't know what you're *talking* about," Ben said.

Uncle Renald cleared his throat. "It's clear Ben rode through the middle of the party, knocking my son Robyn from his horse—"

"I didn't even *see* him there," Ben said. "*Someone* fell off their horse, but it wasn't my fault. The rabbit ran straight at us."

"Ben Lakesbeare rode his cousin down!" Uncle Renald thundered. "Clearly, it was planned. Owen here will swear to it." Poor Owen was sweating, Ben could see.

"Everything got mixed up." Ben looked around. Didn't *anyone* believe him? "Someone slapped my horse, and then it bolted."

"We all saw what *happened*," Cousin Robyn said.

"What is to be done?" Renald appealed to everyone under his fiercely bushy brows. "Did Ben Lakesbeare *intend* to kill his cousin? If so, he must leave his Estates and give up his title."

"To you, I suppose," Ben said.

"What would *you* do with a murderer?" Uncle Renald thrust out his neck. His eyes were glowing dangerously. It was a wild accusation. No one had been murdered yet, except Ben – almost – and that was down to Robyn. Behind him, Ben's mother, Hebe, shook her head.

"A would-be murderer, you mean." Ben took his time. "Let me see." He had the measure of Renald. Instead he turned to Robyn. "Someone who plotted to get rid of his cousin would be the lowest of the low, am I right?"

"Exactly so," Robyn said.

"How about someone who set a trap for his cousin – *the same trap that killed his cousin's father*?"

Uncle Renald coughed sharply.

"A rascal," Robyn said, smoothly. "Beyond help, I'd say. Exile would be too good for him, I think."

"Absolutely," Ben said. "He'd be worthless, wouldn't he? And live *below the salt*." Swiftly Ben took up the glittering bowl of salt that sparkled beside the top table. With a contemptuous look at Robyn, he dashed it down behind him. "There now," he said, "*sweet* Cousin Robyn. You're below it – where you belong!"

"Ben!" Ben's mother said.

"Don't worry, Aunt Hebe." Cousin Robyn brushed salt off his velvet suit. "Ben's hit his head and it's made him say things he doesn't mean."

"How did you know I hit my head?" Ben demanded.

"You said, I mean—"

"No, I didn't. I didn't say anything about it. You only know I hit my head because *you* were there to help me hit it!"

"This is *outrageous*," Renald began. "This boy has overstepped his mark."

"No!" Maudlin said. "He hasn't!"

"*You'll* speak when you're spoken to," Renald growled.

"No!" Maudlin said. "I won't! *I* know what you're up to. I saw it all from the squint. You *planned* the hunt to go wrong. I saw you talking with the Master of Ferrets. I heard you say *Scatter the party* and *Can you do it*, and I knew there was something up!"

"Is no one safe from your prying eyes?" Renald glanced up at the squint.

"No one with bad things to hide. I hate you, Renald. I *won't* be sent away."

"You'll do as you're told."

"I don't think so," Ben said. "Not now I'm twelve next week."

"The Master of Ferrets turned the rabbit and made the horses panic." Nothing could stop Maudlin now. "Renald gave Ben a nervous horse, then you slapped him to make him bolt. It wasn't until I took a walk through the woods after Ben went missing that I found something there that made me—"

"You took a walk through the woods. Without my permission, I take it?" Uncle Renald got up. "Come, Robyn, we don't have to hear this."

Cygnus growled. Her hackles rose. "Stay where you are," Ben said.

Maudlin held something up. "Robyn? I think you dropped this?"

"What?" Robyn flushed. "I don't know. It isn't mine," he said.

"Oh, I think it is. I think you dropped this

knife when you cut the rope you'd tied that big branch back with. The branch that almost killed Ben? It's no use, Uncle Renald. I found the rope as well."

"This knife has your initials on it, Robyn – R.L." Hebe examined it wonderingly.

"That doesn't matter, does it, Father?" Cousin Robyn bleated. "That doesn't prove a thing. It only shows I've *been* there. I haven't *done* anything."

"Robyn, hold your tongue."

"I almost *didn't* do it, anyway. The rope, you know, was so *tough* – "

"Robyn – that will do!"

" – and anyway, Ben's all right now, so what does it matter?"

"Robyn! Enough, I say!"

Renald saw that he was beaten. When at last he raised his head, Ben thought he looked almost sorry.

"Ben Lakesbeare," Renald said, "there is one thing you should know. When you say a trap was laid for you, the *same trap that killed your father*, you should know it isn't true. Your father fell from his horse and broke his head, and no one saw him fall. But no one wished he hadn't more than I. I had nothing to do with your father's death. It was an accident, I swear."

"I hope, for your sake, it was," Ben Lakesbeare said, sternly. He knew exactly what he was doing. It was time to give judgement, he knew.

"Uncle Renald and Cousin Robyn, I must ask you to go from this place. You give up any rights in this House. My aunt Maudlin keeps her dowry and marries whoever she likes. Go now, and take nothing with you, and do not ever return. And leave the black stallion Lascar in my stables."

My beautiful Lascar. *My* stables. Ben Lakesbeare felt cool and lordly and in control. His father's sword and shield looked down from the wall above him. Tomorrow he would have Owen fetch them down and clean them. He knew they belonged to him now.

Chapter 10

Coop

....

"So *there* you are – I thought you were never coming back!" Ben's mother turned and smiled. "We thought you must've fallen down the toilet, but never mind that now. Look who's here. Who do you think? Oh, it's all too exciting!"

"Steady, there, Heather," the tall man next to her said. "One step at a time. Remember, Ben won't know me."

"This – oh, how can I say it?" Ben's mother was all confusion. "This, Ben, is – "

"Better from you than from me," the tall tanned stranger said, and his voice was deep and slow.

" – Ben Laker, this is *your father*!"

"My father?" Ben looked up. The words didn't have any meaning.

"Hi, Ben." The tall man's eyes were anxious. "Ben, I know this is a shock."

"A shock," Ben repeated. It was.

"I've waited for this moment, and now that it's here, I – " The tall man took Ben's hand. His blue eyes looked into Ben's. "Now that it's here, I don't know where to begin. I know," he said slowly, "that I can't just expect to walk back into your life, Ben."

"Thanks for all the ten bucks you sent me on my birthday," Ben said, automatically.

That really hurt, Ben could see.

"It isn't the way I wanted things to be," Ben's father went on. "We lost contact for a long time, your mother and I, but now that I'm over here for good, I'm hoping you'll give me a chance to make it up to you." He looked down as if to say, I know I don't deserve it. He reminded Ben of an old-time knight, with his careful manners and his funny, stiff way of saying things. "If you don't mind my visiting you, that is."

Ben swallowed. He looked at his mum and squeezed her hand hard. "I don't mind, do you?"

"I don't mind visiting, either," Cousin Robin piped up. "I've had a really nice time, Auntie Heather. I could come and stay next holidays, as well. I could come for three weeks next time, if you like, then we could visit more houses and see all history things…"

"I don't know, Robin," Ben's mother tried to say, doubtfully. But Ben's dad had caught her eye.

"I guess we're going to be busy." Ben's father didn't say a lot. But what he *did* say mattered. "We won't have much time for visitors. I guess we've got one heck of a lot of catching up to do."

Robin stared. He'd met his match. "You're my uncle," he said.

"Uncle Cooper." Ben's dad smiled. "You c'n call me Coop."

Coop. It was perfect. "You mean – " Ben looked at his mother " – you mean, he's C. ARRIVES? On the calendar?"

"He's C. ARRIVES on the calendar," Ben's

mother laughed and agreed.

Coop told them all about the funny flight
over he'd had. Then he told them all about
his brand-new job in England, about Ben's
grandparents back in Arkansas, about the
way Ben's grandpa said Huh? and the way
Ben sounded just like him – and all the time
Coop talked, Ben just sat and drank him in.
Suddenly he knew who Coop was. He knew
who *he* was, too. "You're my dad," he said.
Ben hugged and hugged his father, and Coop
just hugged him right back.

"This is a very special evening." Ben's
mother raised her glass. "Let's drink to
Robin's last night."

Ben felt the queen of hearts in his pocket.
Maudlin, he thought. She's all right now. I
bet she married William in the end. She did,
he suddenly knew, because I let her. But she
wasn't at peace until now – until I
remembered doing it.

"And Maudlin," he said, "a friend of mine.
Can we drink to her, too?"

Back in the dark Hall at Pentacote, a face looked down through the squint. The ghosts were laid, the anger was gone, all the wrongs were righted. Her bedroom would always feel calm. Aunt Maudlin looked down and smiled. *"Ben,"* she whispered down five hundred years, *"raise a glass to her now, and Maudlin lives always in your thoughts."*

Ben and Coop raised their glasses. Ben's mother and Robin raised theirs.

"To Maudlin," Coop said, "whoever she is! And Robin – safe journey home!"

C. ARRIVES – ROBIN GOES. What a dad. What a cousin. What a life.

"I'll drink to that," Ben said.

MORE WALKER PAPERBACKS
For You to Enjoy

☐ 0-7445-5203-6   *My Aunty Sal and the Mega-sized Moose*
by Martin Waddell   £3.99

☐ 0-7445-6035-X   *Seven Weird Days at Number 31*
by Judy Allen   £3.99

☐ 0-7445-6018-7   *The Supreme Dream Machine*
by Jon Blake   £3.99

☐ 0-7445-6004-7   *Jeremy Brown of the Secret Service*
by Simon Cheshire   £3.99

☐ 0-7445-6032-2   *Bernard's Gang*
by Dick Cate   £3.99

☐ 0-7445-6012-8   *The Curse of the Skull*
by June Crebbin   £3.99

☐ 0-7445-5223-0   *Smart Girls*
by Robert Leeson   £3.99

Name _____

Address _____

_____